John Foster and Korky Paul

MAGIC POEMS

OXFORD
UNIVERSITY PRESS

Acknowledgements

The editor and publisher are grateful to the following for permission to publish their poems for the first time in this collection:

Andrew Collett, 'The Moon's Magic', Copyright © Andrew Collett 1997.

Paul Cookson, 'Willy the Wizard's Shopping Trip', Copyright © Paul Cookson 1997.

David Harmer, 'Harry Hobgoblin's Superstore' and 'Sir Guy and the Enchanted Princess', Copyright © David Harmer 1997.

Trevor Millum, 'Genie', Copyright © Trevor Millum 1997

Tony Mitton, 'Dreaming the Unicorn', Copyright © A. R. Mitton 1997.

Michaela Morgan, 'Dinner on Elm Street', Copyright © Michaela Morgan 1997.

Jack Ousbey, 'Quickspell the Wizard', Copyright © Jack Ousbey 1997.

Gareth Owen, 'The Magician', Copyright © Gareth Owen 1997.

Marian Swinger, 'The Lonely Enchanter', Copyright © Marian Swinger 1997.

Charles Thomson, 'A Very Modern Witch', Copyright © Charles Thomson 1997.

Jennifer Tweedie, 'Mang, Katong, and the Crocodile King', Copyright © Jennifer Tweedie 1997.

We also acknowledge permission to include previously published poems:

Richard Edwards, 'Maxo, the Magician', Copyright © Richard Edwards 1993, from *Leopards on Mars* (Viking), and 'The Marvellous Trousers', Copyright © Richard Edwards 1987, from *Whispers from a Wardrobe* (Puffin), both reprinted by permission of Felicity Bryan.

Max Fatchen, 'The Ballad of the Waterbed' from *A Paddock of Poems* by Max Fatchen (Omnibus/Puffin, 1987) Copyright © Max Fatchen 1987, reprinted by permission of the author and John Johnson, Ltd.

Shelagh McGee, 'WANTED — A Witch's Cat' from *Smile Please* (Robson Books, 1976), reprinted by permission of the publishers.

Doug MacLeod, 'Miranda, the Queen of the Air' from *The Fed Up Family Album*, reprinted by permission of the publishers, Penguin Books Australia Ltd.

Jack Prelutsky, 'Where Goblins Dwell' from *The Random Book of Poetry for Children*, Copyright © 1983 by Jack Prelutsky, reprinted by permission of Random House, Inc.

For Georgia Bozas K.P.

OXFORD
UNIVERSITY PRESS

Great Clarendon Street, Oxford OX2 6DP

Oxford University Press is a department of the University of Oxford.
It furthers the University's objective of excellence in research, scholarship, and education by publishing worldwide in

Oxford New York
Auckland Cape Town Dar es Salaam Hong kong Karachi Kuala Lumpur Madrid Melbourne Mexico City Nairobi New Delhi Shanghai Taipei Toronto

With offices in

Argentina Austria Brazil Chile Czech Republic France Greece Guatemala Hungary Italy Japan Poland Portugal Singapore South Korea Switzerland Thailand Turkey Ukraine Vietnam

Oxford is a registered trade mark of Oxford University Press in the UK and in certain other countries

First published in 1997
Reissued with a new cover 2004

British Library Cataloguing in Publication Data available

ISBN 978-0-19-276304-4

10 9 8 7 6 5 4

Printed in China

Paper used in the production of this book is a natural, recyclable product made from wood grown in sustainable forests. The manufacturing process conforms to the environmental regulations of the country of origin.

Contents

Where Goblins Dwell

There is a place where goblins dwell,
where leprechauns abound,
where evil trolls inhabit holes,
and elves are often found,
where unicorns grow silver horns,
and mummies leave their tombs,
where fiery hosts of ashen ghosts
cavort in draughty rooms.

There is a place where poltergeists
and ogres rove unseen,
where witches rise through midnight skies,
where stalks the phantom queen,
where fairy folk atop an oak
are apt to weave a spell;
it's there to find within your mind,
that place where goblins dwell.

Jack Prelutsky

Quickspell the Wizard

Quickspell the Wizard, whose fame was immense,
Lived deep in the Forests of Knurld,
Across mountains and oceans his spells and his potions
Were known as the best in the world.

His kaftan and kerchief, his tunic and cone-hat
Were a dazzling sight to behold;
The colours of night, plus polar-bear white
With splashes of scarlet and gold.

But one day this wizard stopped paying attention,
His work was haphazard, slap-dash;
His potion went wrong, it was heated too long
And it blew him away in a flash.

Then wizards appeared from far and from near
From Boinka and Ormoc and Flix,
From Komrat and Rhino, from Pinetop and Yorco
They zoomed in to bury the bits.

On horses with wings, on gliders and things
By carpet and hot-air balloon;
And a wizard called Knockit came in on a rocket,
Returning, by chance, from the moon.

With trombones and tubas, with big drums and cymbals
The band played a song of lament;
The coffin was borne by the Wizards of Zorn
Who were ancient and wizened and bent.

By the side of the grave in the afternoon haze
Stood the priest with his book and his bell,
When a voice from the back said, 'My name is Zak
And I've something important to tell.

My master was Quickspell and some time ago
He worked out a potion unique,
When, if any disaster blew up the Old Master
The spell could be spelled, so to speak.'

And then from his doublet he drew out a goblet
And filled it with potions so rare,
On the cry, 'ZIPPERZODED', the mixture exploded
And a great swirl of snow filled the air.

The wizards all watching, half-blinded and blasted
Were bamboozled, amazed, and aghast
When out of the blizzard stepped Quickspell the Wizard
Restored by the spell Zak had cast.

Then the tubas and tambours, the trombones and oboes
Struck up with a song of delight;
A great fire was built on the side of a hill
And the feasting went on all the night.

Quickspell the Wizard and Zak his apprentice
Still live in the Forests of Knurld;
Across mountains and oceans their spells and their potions
Are known as the best in the world.

Jack Ousbey

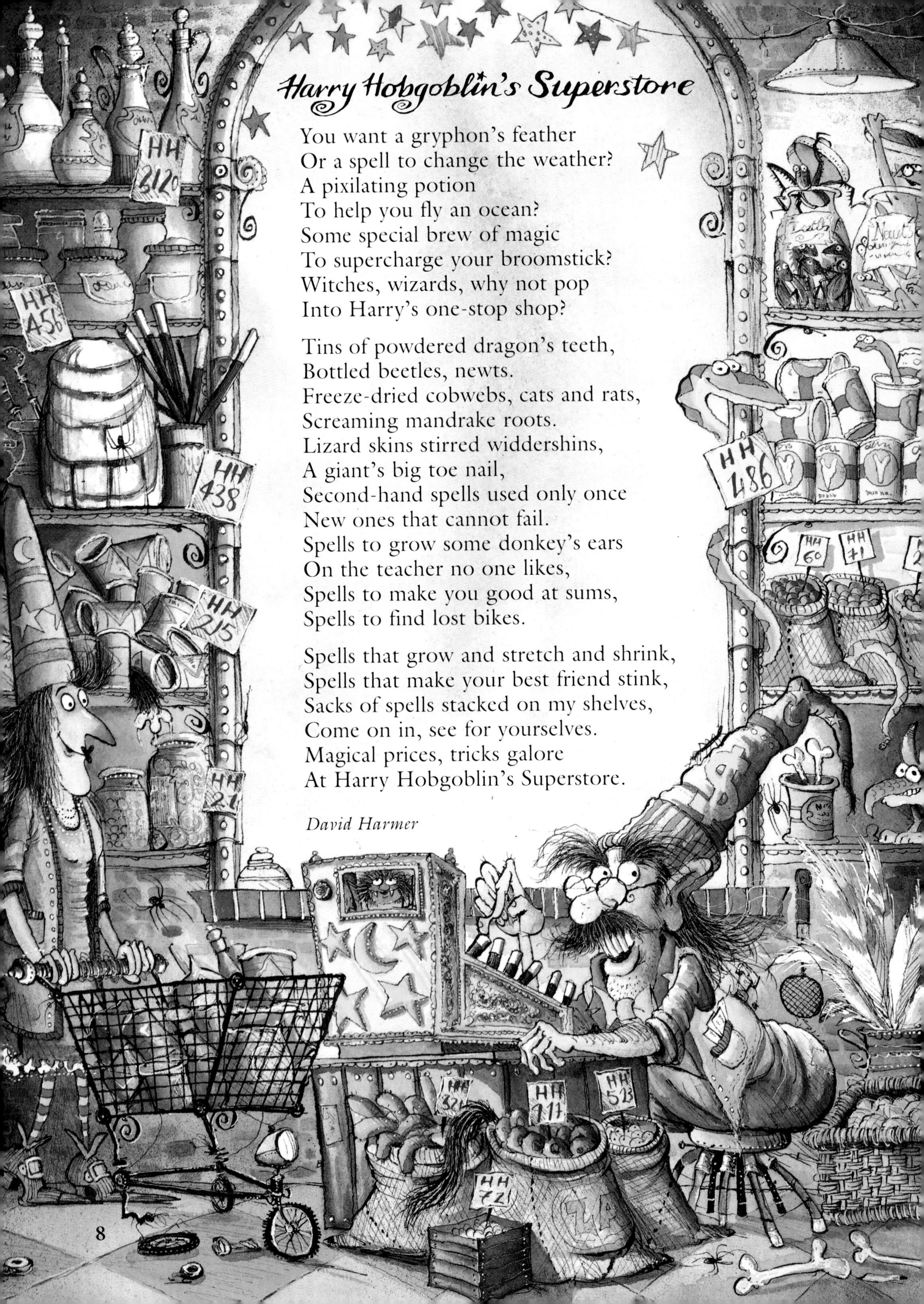

Harry Hobgoblin's Superstore

You want a gryphon's feather
Or a spell to change the weather?
A pixilating potion
To help you fly an ocean?
Some special brew of magic
To supercharge your broomstick?
Witches, wizards, why not pop
Into Harry's one-stop shop?

Tins of powdered dragon's teeth,
Bottled beetles, newts.
Freeze-dried cobwebs, cats and rats,
Screaming mandrake roots.
Lizard skins stirred widdershins,
A giant's big toe nail,
Second-hand spells used only once
New ones that cannot fail.
Spells to grow some donkey's ears
On the teacher no one likes,
Spells to make you good at sums,
Spells to find lost bikes.

Spells that grow and stretch and shrink,
Spells that make your best friend stink,
Sacks of spells stacked on my shelves,
Come on in, see for yourselves.
Magical prices, tricks galore
At Harry Hobgoblin's Superstore.

David Harmer

Willy the Wizard's Shopping Trip

On Saturday, Willy the Wizard
went into town to do his weekly shopping.

He bought vanishing cream from Roots the Alchemist,
a star-spangled cape from Sparks and Mensa,
a new box of tricks from Ploys 'R' Us,
and twenty-four tins of bats' blood soup
from the supermarket — Asda Cadabra!

Then, he met his friend Don Dracula
for a bite at the Burper King,
before picking up a new cauldron
from 'Voodoo It All — The Druid Yourself Store'.

Paul Cookson

Dinner on Elm Street

Thrice the old school cat hath spewed,
Teachers shriek and children whine,
Ring the bell! 'Tis time! 'Tis time!

Round about the cauldron go,
In the mouldy cabbage throw,
Stone-cold custard, thick with lumps,
Germs from Kevin (sick with mumps),
Boil up sprouts for greenish smell,
Add sweaty sock, cheese pie as well.

Froth and splutter, boil and bubble.
March them in here at the double.

Fillet of an ancient steak
In the cauldron boil and bake.
Eye of spud and spawn of frog,
A chocolate moose, a heated dog.
Add the goo from 'twixt the toes
And crusty bits from round the nose.

Froth and splutter, boil and bubble.
March them in here at the double.

Lumpy mincemeat, grey and gristly,
Giblets, gizzards, all things grizzly.
Beak of chicken in a nugget,
With greasy chips the kids will love it.
Scab of knee sprinkle in,
Squeeze juice of pimple from a chin.
Here's the spell to make you thinner,
It's the nightmare Elm Street dinner.

Froth and splutter, boil and bubble.
March them in here at the double!

Michaela Morgan

A Very Modern Witch

I'm a very modern witch
(aged about 300 years)
and I've bought a brand-new broom
with a horn and ninety gears.

I leap into the seat
and turn the laser-key:
the acceleration causes
a thrust of several G.

For mine's the only model
where they have introduced
an extra power source
for triple turbo-boost,

so I can fly from London
to New York or Hong Kong —
and back — before the sound
has faded from a gong.

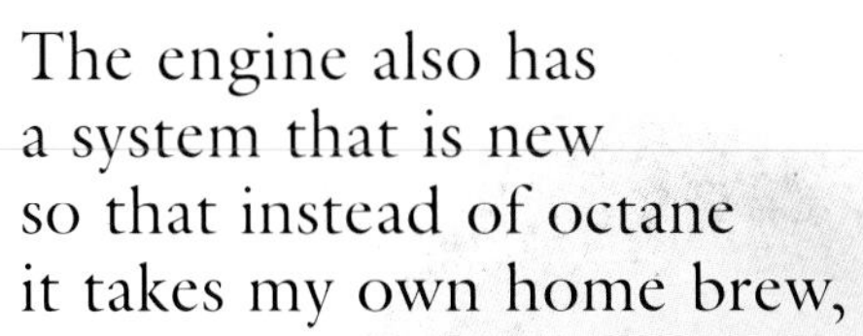

The engine also has
a system that is new
so that instead of octane
it takes my own home brew,

(you know the sort of thing —
dead earwigs, mandrake root,
eggs, hemlock, curried eels,
flat beer and half a boot).

I'm a very modern witch
(aged about 300 years)
and I've bought a brand-new broom
with a horn and ninety gears.

Charles Thomson

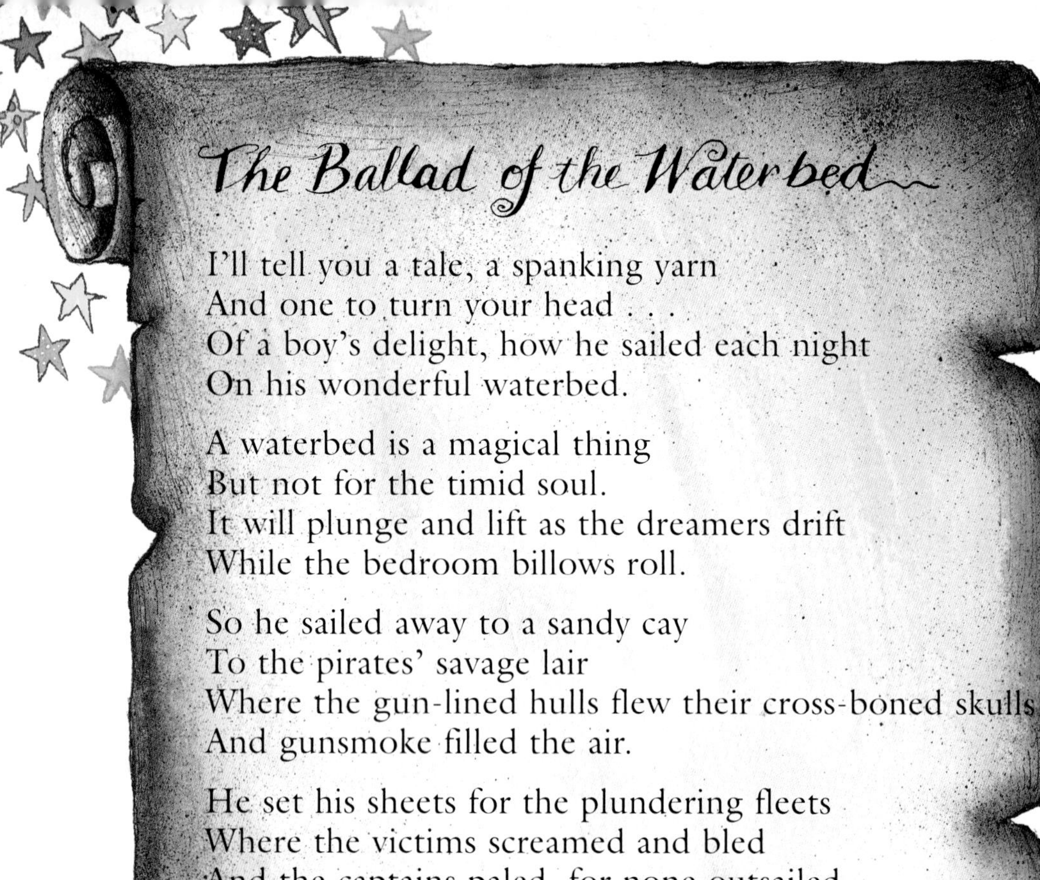

The Ballad of the Waterbed

I'll tell you a tale, a spanking yarn
And one to turn your head . . .
Of a boy's delight, how he sailed each night
On his wonderful waterbed.

A waterbed is a magical thing
But not for the timid soul.
It will plunge and lift as the dreamers drift
While the bedroom billows roll.

So he sailed away to a sandy cay
To the pirates' savage lair
Where the gun-lined hulls flew their cross-boned skulls
And gunsmoke filled the air.

He set his sheets for the plundering fleets
Where the victims screamed and bled
And the captains paled, for none outsailed
That scurvy waterbed.

Fierce Captain Kidd had dipped his lid
And Blackbeard cried, 'It's daft,
I've never seen, in the Caribbean,
The likes of this 'ere craft.'

With a swig of rum for his parrot chum
How Long John Silver roared.
But he quickly sank from a salt-stained plank
When he tried to climb aboard.

So the boy came back when the tide grew slack
To the morning clear and bright,
As he woke he said to the waterbed,
'We sail again tonight.'

So woe to the landlubbers left behind . . .
No treasure or diamond rings
But high and dry with a jealous sigh
On their dull old innersprings.

But I'll tell you this . . . where the bow waves hiss
When the midnight's stroke has gone
Don't risk your neck on a waterbed deck
And keep your lifebelt on!

Max Fatchen

Rum

The Marvellous Trousers

Last week on my way to a friend's birthday tea
I found them draped over the branch of a tree,
Oh, the Marvellous Trousers.

One leg was striped silver, the other striped blue;
I put them on, closed my eyes, wished and then flew!
Oh, the Marvellous Trousers.

They carried me up like a rocket, so fast
I ruffled the tail of each pigeon I passed,
Oh, the Marvellous Trousers.

I soared over Sicily, rolled over Rome,
And circled the Eiffel Tower on my way home,
Oh, the Marvellous Trousers.

I landed with ribbons of cloud in my hair,
But when I looked down at my legs — they were bare!
Oh, no Marvellous Trousers.

I know it sounds funny, I know it sounds weird,
But somehow and somewhere they'd just disappeared,
Oh, the Marvellous Trousers.

And when I explained at my friend's birthday tea,
The guests shook their heads and blew raspberries at me,
Oh, the Marvellous Trousers.

But I don't care tuppence: I've rolled over Rome,
I've circled the Eiffel Tower on my way home,
I've worn the Marvellous Trousers,
The Marvellous, Marvellous Trousers!

Richard Edwards

The Magician

The magician at Daphne's party
Was called The Great Zobezank
But everyone knew he was Daphne's dad
Who worked at the Westminster Bank.

He waved for silence and asked us all
'If there's a volunteer
Who'll step inside my magic box
I'll make you disappear.'

We shouted, 'Mister, please choose me!'
And waved our arms like mad
But he chose Daphne Smart of course
Because he was her dad.

He closed his eyes and raised his wand
And waved it in the air
And when he opened the magic box
Daphne wasn't there.

He bowed and smiled while Daphne's mum
Clapped and we all cheered
Then he uttered the magical words that would make
Daphne re-appear.

But alas when he opened that magic door
No Daphne stood inside
And her father's face turned grey as stone
While her mother wailed and cried.

They called, 'Oh, Daphne please come back!'
And beat upon the door
And as for us we clapped and cheered
Louder than before.

Gareth Owen

Maxo, the Magician

Maxo, the magician,
Was very sharp and slick,
And people flocked from miles around
To see his famous trick,
The one that conjured rabbits,
A hare, two ducks, a cat,
A dozen hens, three foxes
And a goat out of a hat.

Everyone loved Maxo,
They'd 'Bravo!' and applaud,
Yes, everyone loved Max, except
The hat, the hat was bored
And envious — it never got
A single cheer or clap,
And one night at the Hippodrome,
It felt its patience snap.

Maxo, the magician,
Had flashed his brilliant grin,
Had tapped the hat-brim with his wand,
Had started reaching in,
When something startling happened —
He screeched out in alarm,
His hand went in the hat, his wrist,
His elbow, his whole arm,

His cloaked-in-velvet shoulder,
And then, as people cheered,
His head, his chest, his legs and feet
Entirely disappeared.
The audience roared 'Maxo!
Oh, Maxo, sharp and slick,
He's made his whole self vanish
In the hat. Oh, what a trick!'

The curtain fell. The stage-hands
Searched everywhere in vain,
But Maxo, the magician,
Was never seen again.
His dressing-room stands silent now,
And dust lies in his hat,
Which sometimes makes a low
Digestive rumble. Fancy that!

Richard Edwards

Miranda, the Queen of the Air

My Aunty Miranda, a mystic by trade,
Was born in the circus and that's where she stayed.
The people would flock to see Aunty Miranda
Perform with her partner, a Pekingese panda.

'THE QUEEN OF THE AIR' she was fittingly named.
'HER ACT IS UNIQUE!' all the posters exclaimed.
'The Mystic Miranda who comes from the East
Performs levitation on LARGE CHINESE BEASTS!!'

My Aunty Miranda would silence the crowd
And whisper a spell while the panda bear bowed.
Then, after the strange incantation was said
The panda would levitate over her head.

One evening, Miranda misquoted the spell
And there is a plaque where the tragedy fell:
'BELOW LIES MIRANDA, QUEEN OF THE AIR
(Deposed by a plummeting panda bear).'

Doug MacLeod

WANTED — A Witch's Cat

Wanted — a witch's cat.
Must have vigour and spite,
Be expert at hissing,
And good in a fight,
And have balance and poise
On a broomstick at night.

Wanted — a witch's cat.
Must have hypnotic eyes
To tantalize victims
And mesmerize spies,
And be an adept
At scanning the skies.

Wanted — a witch's cat,
With a sly, cunning smile,
A knowledge of spells
And a good deal of guile,
With a fairly hot temper
And plenty of bile.

Wanted — a witch's cat,
Who's not afraid to fly,
For a cat with strong nerves
The salary's high.
Wanted — a witch's cat;
Only the best need apply.

Shelagh McGee

Genie

Up in granny's attic, full of ancient junk:
Albums and gramophones and an old wooden trunk.
Peering in the dark — ouch! — ker-clunk!

Tripped over something and hurt my shin
Bruised my leg on this lamp of tin
Then . . . heard a whistling from within!

'Excuse the crutch and the leg in plaster;
What do you desire from me, O master?'

Oh, no. Just my luck to get
the Genie of the Magic L~~a~~imp.

I banged my head against the wall:
Stars, flashing lights — I saw them all
And heard a deep and magical call:

'Forgive the bandage and the swollen head;
How can I help?' the Genie said.

Oh no. This time I've got
the Genie of the Magic L~~a~~ump.

So . . . I rubbed the lamp with special care
'Genie, Genie, come out of there!'
A whoosh and a whizz and a puff of air!

'I'm the Genie of the Magic Lamp,' I heard it say.
'At last,' I said. 'A proper Genie's come my way.
What shall I do to make it stay?'

'A Genie of wisdom, a sage from afar,
Please speak to me, whoever you are!'
But
When it finally spoke, it just said 'Baa!'

Baa?
Oh no, I think perhaps I misheard the name
I've got the Genie of the Magic Lam~~p~~b!

Trevor Millum

Sir Guy and the Enchanted Princess

Through howling winds on a storm-tossed moor
Sir Guy came to a castle door.

He was led by some strange power
To the deepest dungeon of a ruined tower.

A Princess sat on a jewelled throne
Her lovely features carved in stone.

His body trembled, was she dead?
Then her sweet voice filled his head.

'These evil spirits guard me well,
Brave Sir Knight, please break their spell.

Though I am stone, you shall see,
Kiss me once, I shall be free.'

As demons howled she came to life
Blushed and whispered, 'Have you a wife?'

'My love,' he said, 'still remains
With collecting stamps and spotting trains.

But as long as you do as you're told,
I think you'll do, come on it's cold.'

'Oh,' she cried, 'you weedy bore
I wish I was entranced once more.'

Lightning struck, the demons hissed,
Sir Guy was stone, a voice croaked, 'Missed!'

The Princess rode his horse away
And poor Sir Guy's still there today.

David Harmer

Mang, Katong, and the Crocodile King

Deep in the jungle,
in the land of Mangoree,
lived Mang, the magic drummer,
in a frangipani tree.
Boom-kiri, boom-kiri, boom-boom-kiree.

A boy called Katong
from the village, came to sing,
'Mang, make your magic
melt the Crocodile King.'
Boom-kiri, boom-kiri, boom-boom-karing.

'The Crocodile King
has eaten my ma,
chewed up my gran
and swallowed my pa.'
Boom-kiri, boom-kiri, boom-boom-karaa.

'You are small,' said Mang,
'but you want a great thing.
It will be hard to melt
the Crocodile King.'
Boom-kiri, boom-kiri, boom-boom-karing.

'I will help,' said Katong.
And he beat on the drum
while Mang made his magic,
'Basoko, bagum.'
Boom-kiri, boom-kiri, boom-boom-katum.

Then sparks flew up
from their beating hands
and went whizzing and sizzling
all over the land,
like fireworks made
from the sun and moon,
until they lit up King Croc
in the village lagoon.
Boom-kiri, boom-kiri, boom-boom-boom.

The villagers cheered,
'Hooray! hooray!'
as they saw the sparks melt
King Crocodile away.
Boom-kiri, boom-kiri, boom-boom-kiray.

'He's gone,' cried Katong.
'Now my village is free!'
And Mang said, 'Katong,
come and live with me.
We'll both make magic
in my frangipani tree,
deep in the jungle
in the land of Mangoree.'
Boom-kiri, boom-kiri, boom-boom-karee.

Jennifer Tweedie

Dreaming the Unicorn

I dreamed I saw the Unicorn
last night.
It rippled through the forest,
pearly white,
breathing a moonlit silence.

Its single horn
stood shining like a lance.
I saw it toss its head
and snort and prance
and paw the midnight air.
Its mane was like a mass
of silver hair.

But suddenly it shuddered.
It sensed my spellbound gaze,
my wondering eyes,
and turned to look upon me with surprise,
seeming to read my face
and looking as if to say,
'You are not from this place.
What is your business here?'

My mind was far from clear.
I could not think or speak.
Above my head, I heard the branches creak
and then, from where I stood,
I watched it flicker off into the wood,
into the velvet space between the trees.

A sudden rush of rapid midnight breeze,
that felt both chill and deep,
awoke me from my sleep,
and there upon the pillow by my head
I found a strand of shining silver thread.

I kept that strand of mane,
I keep it, still,
inside a box upon my window sill.
And when the world hangs heavy
on my brain,
it helps me dream the Unicorn again.

Tony Mitton

The Moon's Magic

When the moon fell in the ocean
stretching long and wide,
sailing ships all came to see
its magic deep inside.

They came to see its mountains
to touch its secret stone,
but most of all they came to catch
its magic for their own.

They came with giant hammers
to crack its magic face,
they came with ropes and fishing nets
to tie it into place.

They came with swords and daggers
to tear the moon apart,
they came with iron bars
to break its silver heart.

They filled their ships with plenty
they piled its magic light,
until the moon, stretching wide,
vanished in the night.

And as they clapped and cheered
for a job they'd done so well,
they disappeared, like magic,
into a midnight spell.

So if you ever notice
the moon long and wide,
walk up close, catch a glimpse
of its magic deep inside.

But before you stop to wonder
for a magic of your own,
watch the moon sinking low
with its sailing ships of stone.

Andrew Collett

The Lonely Enchanter

Alone, the enchanter stands,
tall, dark and grim.
His servants, the peasants,
are frightened of him.
He watches the world
from his great castle tower.
Enchantments and magic
have given him power.
They've given him treasure
and wealth without end.
'All this,' he says sadly,
'but never a friend.'

Marian Swinger